For my mom and dad, and for anyone who
has risked something to live authentically
—DH

To anyone who has ever felt different or
out of place; you are beautiful and you are loved
—SL

A PROUD PARTNERSHIP BETWEEN

glaad + little bee books

A portion of the proceeds from the sale of this
book will be donated to accelerating
LGBTQ acceptance.

little bee books

New York, NY
Text copyright © 2021 by Daniel Haack
Illustrations copyright © 2021 by Stevie Lewis
Manufactured in China RRD 1220
littlebeebooks.com
First Edition
10 9 8 7 6 5 4 3 2 1
Library of Congress Cataloging-in-Publication Data
Names: Haack, Daniel, author. | Lewis, Stevie, illustrator.
Title: Tale of the Shadow King / words by Daniel Haack; pictures by Stevie Lewis.
Description: First edition. | New York, NY: Little Bee Books, [2021] |
Series: Prince & Knight | Audience: Ages 4-8. | Audience: Grades K-1. |
Summary: When a dark and mysterious Shadow King causes a fog of darkness
to spread across their kingdom, the prince and the knight, now happily
married, set out to find and stop him.
Identifiers: LCCN 2020047537 | Subjects: CYAC: Stories in rhyme. | Princes—Fiction.
Knights and knighthood—Fiction. | Kings, queens, rulers, etc.—Fiction. |
Gays—Fiction. | Classification: LCC PZ8.3.H1125 Tal 2021 | DDC [E] —dc23
LC record available at https://lccn.loc.gov/2020047537

ISBN 978-1-4998-1121-6
For information about special discounts on bulk purchases,
please contact Little Bee Books at sales@littlebeebooks.com.

Prince & Knight
TALE OF THE SHADOW KING

words by **Daniel Haack**   pictures by **Stevie Lewis**

little bee books

Have you heard the thrilling tale
of the prince and his dear knight?

Their love for one another
inspired everyone in sight.

The sun shined on their union,
and it beamed as they were crowned.

The whole realm felt its warmth,
from the treetops to the ground.

Yet while their kingdom prospered
and grew under their care,
a fog of darkness spread,
sending chills throughout the air.

It started with just a wisp
that slowly veiled the sky.
But when daylight did not return,
the prince and knight could not stand by.

The shadow ha destroyed our crops,
and we're starving from this blight."

The prince said to his husband,
"We must face this threat tonight!"

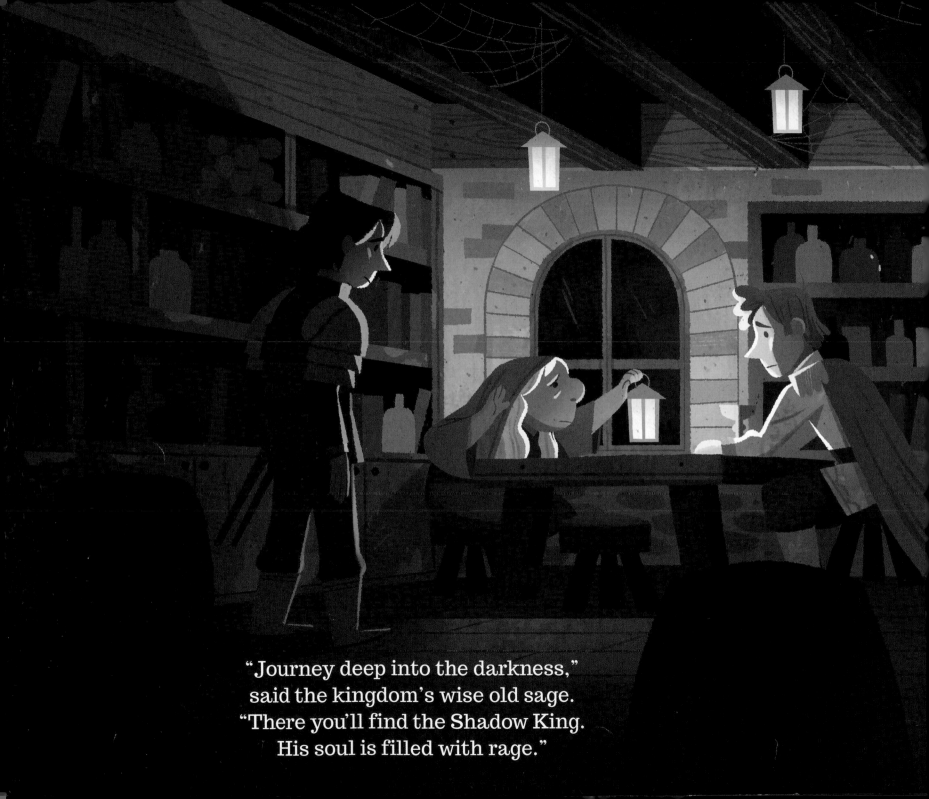

"Journey deep into the darkness,"
said the kingdom's wise old sage.
"There you'll find the Shadow King.
His soul is filled with rage."

"Some people say he's evil,
so heed their words of advice.
Be careful if you meet him,
or you will surely pay a price!"

So the prince and knight set off,
their warriors by their side,
trudging through the wilderness
with flaming torches as their guide.

They found the King's foul fortress
past a wide and rushing river.
"Let's be careful as we cross,"
said the knight with quite a shiver.

They jumped from rock to rock,
but before they reached the shore,
monsters thundered toward them!
The troop was now at war!

It took all their strength to fight them,
until there was one last beast.
It started racing at the prince . . .
it was looking for a feast!

The knight blocked the villain's path
and knocked it to the side.
But the knight had lost his footing,
and he fell into the tide.

The prince quickly dove right in
to save the knight before he drowned.

He swam with speed and pulled him out.
His one true love was safe and sound.

The knight kissed the prince and said,
"You put your own life on the line."

As you did for me," said the prince.
"I know you'll always be mine."

The Shadow King was watching.
He fell down to his knees.
"I wish to end this darkness!
Don't hurt me, I beg you, please!"

"I used to be so happy," he said
as a tear streamed down his cheek.
"But soon the world turned against me,
for the way I dress and speak."

"Because I loved a squire, I was banished to the dark.
As the sadness grew inside me, I felt these powers spark."

"It's unfair how you were treated,"
the humble knight replied.
"Our differences make us unique.
Let's celebrate them with pride."

"I'm sorry you've been told these things
should cause you worry and shame.
Like the colors of the rainbow,
I'm glad we're not all the same."

"I believed I wasn't worthy,"
the King said to the men.
"But when I see the love you share,
I'm filled with hope again."

It was the first time in so long
the King had felt this warm.
Light radiated around him;
he felt himself transform.

"Would you like to come with us?"
the prince asked, and took his hand.

And with this loving touch,
sunlight spread across the land.

He was welcomed to their home
and built his own family.

"How wonderful life is," he cried,
"when I can truly be me."